W9-AVE-067

This book belongs to

_____

_____

Aged _____

THE
Bottom of the Garden

AND OTHER STORIES

THE
Bottom of the Garden

AND OTHER STORIES

p

This is a Parragon Publishing Book
This edition published in 2001

Parragon Publishing
Queen Street House
4 Queen Street
Bath BA1 1HE, UK

Copyright © Parragon 2000

ISBN 0-75254-745-3

Designed by Mik Martin

Printed in Italy

These stories have been previously
published by Parragon in the
Bumper Bedtime Series

CONTENTS

The Bottom of the Garden

Written by Candy Wallace

DID YOU KNOW there are probably fairies living at the bottom of your garden? It's the perfect place, with lots of tangly weeds, upturned flowerpots and old trees with handy holes in the trunk. And people seldom visit the bottom of their gardens. "I'm going to dig a nice vegetable patch down there this spring," they say, but they never do.

There was once a very old house that had been empty for years, so the entire garden was as wild as a jungle.

The lawn had been neat, short and bright green. Now the grass was so high it waved to you in the breeze and was tangled with wild flowers, nettles and prickly brambles that crept along the ground.

It all looked neglected and unloved to the human eye. But it was full of life — butterflies loved the wild flowers, little dormice

nested in the grass, birds loved all the juicy worms and grubs to be had and, though you couldn't see them, the garden was the home of some other little creatures, too.

Until, that is, the new owners moved in.

One fine morning, a great big van and a red car drew up outside the old house and stopped. Out of the car scrambled a little girl and her parents.

The grown-ups started to move furniture and boxes into the house from the van, while the little girl, whose name was Lucy, decided to explore. It was just about the most exciting thing in the world to move to this lovely old house with its big garden surrounded by a wall. And Dad had promised her a swing! She walked around the side of the house to look at the garden and gasped when she saw the overgrown chaos. She sat down on a crumbling step, put her chin in her hands and tried to imagine it all tidied up with her swing in the corner.

"Excuse me," said a tiny voice. Lucy sat up straight and blinked. That was the trouble with daydreaming, you imagined all kinds of strange things.

"I'm up here," said the little voice again. "On the bird table."

Lucy squinted and rubbed her eyes. There seemed to be a very tiny person with flower petals on her head, sitting on the rickety bird table and swinging her legs.

She looked very like a picture of a fairy in one of Lucy's books. But of course, she couldn't be, because there were no such thing as fairies.

"Are you lot moving in?" said the voice,

"because this is our garden and we don't want it spoiled by people with big boots and spades and lawnmowers and weedkillers..."

Lucy blinked again. "Yes, we are," she replied. "Are you really

a fairy? How very exciting!
Wait here a minute and I'll fetch
my mum and dad — they'll never
believe me!"

"No point," said the little fairy.
"Grown-ups can't see or hear
fairies. Only children. Sorry."

"How can you live here?" asked
Lucy. "It's horrible!"

The fairy looked cross.

"Most of us live either in the
flowerpots, or the molehills or in
the tree trunks or in old birds'
nests. They're very cosy — I'm
moving into one myself soon."

"Lucy!" called Dad, as he
opened the back door and came
into the garden. "Don't you worry

about your swing. I'll soon knock this garden into shape." He beamed at her. "I'm going to clear the whole garden and lay a new lawn. I thought your swing could go over in that corner." With that he went back into the house to help the removal men.

Lucy turned around to see the fairy sitting on her shoulder, looking miserable.

"This is terrible," said the fairy. "This garden has been our home for years. All our best friends are here, the butterflies, birds, dormice and bees. We'll all have to find somewhere else to live. But goodness knows where." As Lucy listened, little fairy figures hopped down from twigs and flowers, clambered out from under toadstools and popped their heads over the top of cracked flowerpots.

"Can you help us?" asked one.

"All the other gardens are spick and span around here. Where will we go?" said another.

Lucy's mother called to her from the house. It was time to sort out her new bedroom.

"I expect I dreamed all this, because I don't believe in fairies," said Lucy. "But if I didn't and you really are fairies and this garden really is your home, I promise I'll think of something to help you.

I promise!" And with that she jumped up and ran into the house.

Over the next week or so, everyone worked really hard to clean the house. There was no time to clear the garden. Until one day, when a new garden shed and a shiny new set of gardening tools were delivered.

"I can't wait to start on this garden!" said Dad rubbing his hands with glee. "You'll soon have your swing up, Lucy!" and off he went to look at his new shed.

Lucy felt terrible. She still hadn't thought of a plan to save the fairies! If she didn't come up with something soon, they'd be homeless, and all the other creatures too!

She sat in her bedroom, gazing out at the garden and watching a

fairy collecting cobwebs outside her window. A butterfly fluttered by and settled on the window ledge.

"I know!" cried Lucy suddenly. "I know just what to do!" That evening, Lucy ate her tea with her mum and dad. "Dad," she said, in between mouthfuls of toast. "I've had a lovely idea for the garden."

"Don't talk to me about the garden," said Dad, gloomily. "It's going to take me forever to tidy it. It took me all day just to clear a corner for the shed."

"Well, I've had an idea," replied Lucy. "Why don't we leave the bottom half as a wildlife garden? Then the lovely wild flowers and all the butterflies and birds and — er — other little creatures —will still have a home!"

"That's a nice idea, Lucy," said Mum. Dad cheered-up immediately. Only half the work to do! So that's what they did. When Dad decided

to make a pond in the wildlife garden that summer, only Lucy, sitting on her new swing, could see dozens of tiny creatures diving off the lily pads into the water and rowing tiny apple leaf boats. Little frogs soon moved in and water boatmen and dragonflies, too. In fact, Lucy's wildlife garden teemed with life, some of which the grown-ups would never, ever see.

The Tooth Fairy

Written by Candy Wallace

IT ALL BEGAN when Thomas Timpson went to tea with his Grandma. Thomas's Grandma made very nice teas — well, almost! She made little squidgy sandwiches and wibbly-wobbly green jellies and strawberry milkshakes so frothy you got pink bubbles on the end of your nose. And she made rock cakes. Grandma's rock cakes were like — um — rocks. If you dropped one, Grandma's best china shook and rattled on the sideboard and her cat, Tibbles, ran in terror to hide under the sofa.

One day, when Thomas Timpson went to tea and bit into one of Grandma's rock cakes, his

wobbly tooth came out and dropped onto his plate with a clink.

"Lucky Thomas!" said Grandma.
"Let me put that tooth in a napkin
for you. You must take it home and
put it under your pillow for the
Tooth Fairy!"

When Grandma disappeared
into the kitchen, Thomas quickly

popped the rest of his rock cake in the plant pot where Grandma's aspidistra grew. That's where he always put his rock cakes.

Thomas wasn't too sure about this Tooth Fairy business, but he was prepared to give it a try. So that night he put his tooth under his pillow and went to sleep.

The next morning, Thomas was amazed to find that his tooth had gone — and there was a shiny new coin lying in its place!

Thomas couldn't understand why anybody would want his old tooth, but he was very glad to have the coin. When he emptied his money-box he discovered there was nearly enough now to buy a new football!

The next week, to his delight, Thomas found that he had another wobbly tooth. He wiggled and jiggled it, but it just wouldn't budge.

"Mum," said Thomas, "please can I go to tea with Grandma?"

Grandma was pleased to see Thomas again. "I've made you some of your favourite rock cakes!" she said.

"What does the Tooth Fairy do with children's teeth, Grandma?" said Thomas, munching on a cheese and cucumber sandwich.

"You'll have to ask the Tooth Fairy," Grandma chuckled and went to get a fresh batch of rock cakes out of the oven.

"Now you tuck into those dear," said Grandma, "while I water my aspidistra. It's not looking at all well nowadays..."

Thomas closed his eyes tight and bit bravely into a cake. Hey, presto! Out came the tooth!

That night, Thomas didn't put the tooth under his pillow but instead decided to take Grandma's advice. He wrote a note which said:

"Dear Tooth Fairy, I do have a tooth for you but it's hidden. Wake me up and I'll tell you where it is. What do you want it for? Love, Thomas."

And he settled down and went to sleep. He was in the middle of a horrible dream where a giant rock cake with big teeth was trying to eat him, when he suddenly woke up. He was amazed to see a tiny creature on his pillow, with miniature spectacles on her nose, reading his note and tutting to herself.

Thomas rubbed his eyes to make sure he wasn't still dreaming.

"Excuse me," he said, "are you the Tooth Fairy?"

"Yes I am, and after tonight I'm going to ask for a transfer to Dingly Dell duty. Dancing round a couple of toadstools is going to be a piece of cake after this job."

"I'll tell you where my tooth is if you tell me what you're going to use it for," said Thomas firmly.

"In my day children kept quiet and did as they were told," said the fairy, looking very cross. She put her spectacles away in a tiny pocket and folded her arms. "All right, it's a deal."

Thomas took his tooth from his bedside drawer and gave it to the fairy.

"But I don't have time to explain," she said. "You'll have to come and see for yourself."

Thomas was thrilled. "Will you whisk me off to Fairyland with a magic wand?" he asked excitedly,

remembering the school play.
Janice Potts had a wand to go with
her fairy costume made out of a
stick with a silver star on the end.

"You're a bit behind the times,"
sniffed the fairy, taking out a tiny
remote control that sparkled in the
moonlight. She pointed it at Thomas
and pressed the button...

"WOW!" Thomas was standing
in a vast room that sparkled and
shone, as though covered with
silvery cobwebs. In the middle of
the room was a huge machine with
a giant funnel at the top and a
moving conveyor belt beneath.
At the top of the funnel a big
swinging bucket was filling up and

emptying its cargo into the funnel. From the other end came a fine, sparkly powder that reflected all the colours of the rainbow. It flowed like a river along the conveyor belt to where it was dropped into little sacks and sealed.

Hundreds of fairies were busy everywhere, scurrying away with the sacks to load them onto little trollies, counting and making notes, bringing more supplies for the funnel. Dozens of little lights flashed on and off.

"See that funnel?" said the Tooth Fairy. "That's where your tooth will go. All the little teeth are dropped into there and what comes out the other end is magic powder. It's the secret ingredient in lots of our spells. We used pearls in the old days, but they're rather difficult to get hold of now."

"So now you use teeth!" exclaimed Thomas.

"Teeth are very valuable to us fairies," said the Tooth Fairy. "That's why we always pay you."

Thomas gazed in amazement at the sparkling scene. Magic powder hung in the air all around. When he looked down at his hand, it glittered in the silvery light.

"I have to take tonight's teeth to the stores," said the Fairy, "and you must go back before morning. But since you're here, I'll grant you three wishes. We had cut wishes down to two, but we've got a special offer on at the moment. Thomas could hardly believe his ears. He closed his eyes and took a deep breath.

"I wish that I could buy my new football ... and I wish that Grandma's rock cakes were light and fluffy ... and I wish that her aspidistra would get better..."

Before he could finish speaking, the fairy factory had vanished. He was lying in his bed with the sun. shining through his window. Feeling under the pillow, he felt a coin! Thomas rushed to his piggy bank and shook out all the money. He counted carefully. Yes! There was enough for the new football!

He took it round to Grandma's the following week when he went for tea. "Very nice, dear," said

Grandma, as she brought in some delicious-smelling rock cakes fresh from the oven. Thomas sank his teeth into one and took a big bite. It was soft and crumbly, and full of big, juicy currants.

"These are great, Grandma!" he said in a mumbly sort of way because his mouth was full.

"Thank you, dear. It's a new recipe. Now you tuck in while I water my aspidistra — it's coming on a treat."

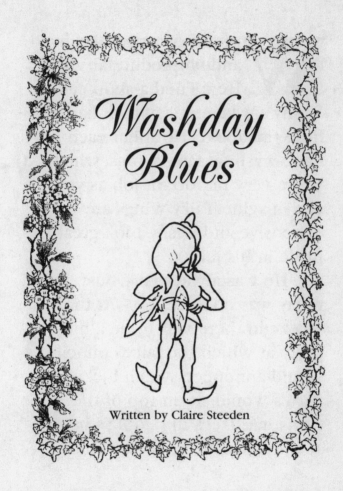

Washday Blues

Written by Claire Steeden

WISHY WASHY the fairy lived and worked in fairyland. He owned a shop called Wishy's Washeteria, which had a little flat above. He spent each day hand-washing fairy wings, which was a very important job as you can imagine. Fairy wings are very expensive and Wishy took great pride in his job.

He was always very busy and today was no exception. At the weekend there was to be a huge party at which the fairy council would announce which lucky fairies would sit on top of the Christmas trees in people's homes at Christmas time. All day long fairies were coming in with sets of wings and asking if they would be ready by Saturday, as they wanted to look their best.

"Oh, I'll never wash all these wings in time," Wishy said to himself. "Each pair takes so long to do. It's Thursday afternoon already."

Wishy lifted a pair of wings gently into the tub, filled with warm water. He picked up a packet

of Fairiel washing powder to sprinkle over the wings, but realized that it was empty.

"Oh, bother. That's all I need. Now what am I going to do? I've got a whole pile of wings to wash and no powder. I'll never have it all done by Saturday."

Wishy remembered seeing an advertisement in the newspaper for washing machines. "Maybe it's time I bought one," he thought. He found the paper and read the advertisement aloud.

"No more wash-day blues. Put a whizz into your wash with a brand new washing machine and let it work while you play!"

"Perfect. That's just what I need." Wishy phoned the company and they sent a fairy round to install one right away.

"Just read the instruction booklet and it will tell you how it works," said the plumber fairy, handing him a big box of powder.

"Thank you. I'll soon get all this washing done now," said Wishy.

After saying goodbye he went to look at his new machine. It was very big and covered in buttons and flashing lights. Wishy sat down and started to read the instructions, but they were far too complicated.

"It'll take me ages to work all of this out. If I just put it on a simple program it should be okay," Wishy said to himself. "Besides, I've got and important evening ahead and I must go and get ready. It's the final of the fairyland quiz competition tonight. If I win I can spend the money on a holiday. I haven't had one for years."

Wishy took all the wings off their hangers, loaded them into the machine, put in some of the new powder and set the machine on what he thought was a low setting. Then off he flew to the quiz, hoping to win the star prize so he could travel to the mountains.

Wishy took his seat just as the contest began. The host asked the contestants lots of questions, and to his surprise, Wishy ended up in the final three, with one tie-breaker question to answer:

"What," asked the fairy host, "is the highest mountain in Fairyland?"

"Mount Sparkle," answered Wishy.

"Correct. You've won the competition and a thousand fairy pieces!"

Everyone cheered, especially Wishy. He could have a holiday at last! He could not believe his luck. A lovely new washing machine and winning the competition all in one day! And to think he had been so miserable this morning.

Arriving home, he took off his wings and was just climbing into bed when he heard an awful rumbling noise coming from downstairs. Pulling on his dressing gown, Wishy went to investigate. The noise seemed to be coming from the laundry. Nervously, he stepped into the dark room.

"Yuk! What's that?" Wishy's feet were covered in something cold and tickly. He turned on the light and looked around. He couldn't believe his eyes. The whole floor was covered in soap suds, which were pouring out of his new machine. He ran to turn it off.

"Oh my goodness! What a

mess. I hope the wings are all right," he said, opening the machine's door.

First of all he pulled out a pair that were enormous. "Oh, no. They've stretched. This pair is ruined. Oh dear!"

He reached in and pulled out another pair which looked the right size, but when he held them up they were full of holes. "Oh dear. They're all torn. I won't be able to mend holes that size," he sighed.

Suds were still oozing out onto the floor as he reached in and pulled out a bundle of wings. As he untangled them he let out a groan. "Ooh, all the colours have run. The new automatic powder I used can't have been right for these wings. The colours have mixed and made the wings patchy. What a disaster!" he cried.

Tears welled up in Wishy's eyes as he pulled out the last pair of wings. They were tiny.

"Oh dear. The water must have got too hot. It's shrunk this pair."

Wishy sat on his little wooden stool and cried, but his tears were

lost amongst the bubbles. "All the wings are ruined and the fairies need them for Saturday. What am I going to do?" he wept.

Wishy spent all night clearing up the soapy mess.

"This will teach me not to be impatient. If I'd washed them by hand I wouldn't be in this mess," he said to himself. "I can't repair the wings, so I'll have to give each customer the money to buy a new pair. I'll have to use the money I won in the competition last night."

Wishy spent all the next day explaining to his customers about the machine and their ruined wings. After handing out money all day he only had twenty fairy pieces left of his prize money.

"At least everyone will have lovely new wings for tomorrow night.I can always go on holiday next year," sighed wishy.

On Saturday morning the plumber fairy came to take the washing machine away again. Wishy decided he would always to do his washing by hand in future.

That night all the fairies gathered at the grand hall to find out who would be chosen to decorate the Christmas trees. Everyone looked magnificent in their sparkly outfits and shiny new wings.

At eight o'clock a list of names was announced and there was much celebrating amongst the fairies. Just as Wishy was about to leave he heard his name being called out, and he turned to face the fairy speaker.

"Wishy, I understand that it is thanks to you that the fairies all have such beautiful new wings this evening," she said. "I hear you had an accident with your new washing machine, and you spent all the prize money you won in the quiz competition buying new wings for everybody. A thousand fairy pieces is a lot of money. I understand you wanted to spend it on a holiday in the mountains," said the fairy.

"Yes, that's right," replied Wishy.

"Well, you have proved what a hard working, kind and honest fairy you are. Your behaviour deserves some kind of reward." The fairy speaker handed Wishy an envelope. "Here's some money that your friends and customers have collected for you. Everyone thinks you deserve a holiday, so you will make it to the mountains after all! Enjoy your trip."

Wishy thanked everybody, and when he got home he thought how lucky he was to have his little shop, such caring friends, and a lovely holiday to look forward to.

Fairy Dust Dilemma

Written by Dave King

FLORENCE WAS NOT a happy fairy. She had spent the whole day turning her house upside down. Not literally, of course, as that would cause more problems than it solved. No, Florence had been searching through cupboards and drawers, looking in boxes and digging into nooks and crannies. All in pursuit of one particular and very special thing ... fairy dust!

Now Florence had not been a fairy for very long. In fact she had onlv graduated from the School for Gifted Fairies, Elves and Pixies a matter of weeks ago, which was all the more reason why her present predicament was so embarrassing.

If she was an old fairy, she would perhaps have some excuse for her forgetfulness. But to have forgotten where or how to make fairy dust so soon after graduating . . . well, she would probably never live it down if anyone ever found out. The day had begun well enough. Florence had been flitting around the flower beds of one of the local parks, making sure that all the flowers were tended to (Florence, you see, was a fully qualified Flower Fairy).

Just as she was taking off from a particularly high daffodil — fairies aren't very tall, don't forget — she suddenly felt a very peculiar, tingling sensation. And with that, she fell to the ground, landing in a patch of muddy soil. As a rule, fairies don't like getting muddy and Florence was no exception. In fact, she positively hated it!

Florence sat grumpily in the mud, wondering what could possibly have made her fall. She got up, brushed herself down as best she could and leapt daintily into the air once more ... only to land, splat, face first in the mud!

"Oh bother!" she said (although, with a mouthful of mud it sounded more like "Bob blobber!" which, if you ask me, is a very peculiar thing to say).

For some reason it seemed she was unable to fly, so Florence began to walk home. She looked a fine sight, covered from head to foot with mud. Florence wished she could clean the mud off and, as if in answer to her wishes, it began to rain. It came down gently at first, almost a fine mist, but by the time Florence reached home, it was pouring down in torrents.

Florence walked into her house and plopped down on the stairs, feeling very miserable.

"I'm feeling very miserable!" she stated, to no one in particular. Fairies have a nasty habit of stating the obvious.

Once she had dried herself off and changed her clothes, Florence moved into the kitchen and went over to the bookshelf.

"Now where did I put that book?" she said. "I was only looking at it yesterday, so it can't have gone too far!" The book in question was the Big Book of Fairy Facts, Figures, Spells, Potions and Cookery Tips, a very useful book which no self-respecting fairy would be seen dead without.

"I simply have to find it!" Florence snapped, as she stomped from one room to another. And then she remembered, she had been reading the book whilst taking a bath! She rushed upstairs to the bathroom and then remembered something else ... she had dropped the book into the bath. It lay on the window ledge. Some of the pages had stuck together and the rest had gone quite crinkly, but she was still able to find the section she was looking for.

She read through the section

on flight most intently. Eventually, she leapt up. "Ah ha!" she said. "Fairy dust, of course! How could I forget?" Fairy dust was the magic substance which gave fairies the power of flight, amongst other things. "Now then," she said, "all I have to do is find the section on how to make fairy dust! I hope I've got the right ingredients."

She flipped through the book, only to discover that the chapter on fairy dust was well and truly stuck together, and no amount of prising, pulling, tugging or tearing was going to pull the pages apart. "Oh, puddlesticks!" Florence shouted, stamping her feet.

Not having the slightest clue as to what she should do next, Florence stomped back downstairs. "This is stupid!" she thought. "A fairy who can't fly is as much use as . . . as . . . well, as something that is probably pretty useless!"

She began to pace around in little, nervous circles. If anyone were to hear about this, she could find herself barred from the Guild of Fairies. She'd become an outcast in Fairyland, she might even have to go and live amongst the trolls, and we all know how bad that would be!

"Perhaps I can find some fairy dust lying around the house!"

Florence exclaimed. She began to run from room to room, throwing open cupboards, emptying out the contents of drawers onto the floor, climbing on chairs to look in high places and getting down on her hands and knees to look in low places. She looked in the attic and she looked in the cellar, but no matter how hard she looked, she simply could not find what she was looking for. Of course, it might have helped if she could have remembered just what fairy dust looked like. It has to be said that Florence really was a rather forgetful fairy.

Florence burst into tears.

"Waaaaaaaahhh!!" she cried.
Just then, the doorbell went.
Florence looked horrified. She
didn't want anyone to see her like
this, so she tidied herself up and
answered the door.

It was her best friend, Phyllis.
"Hello!" Phyllis said. "And how
are..." was all she managed to say
before Florence grabbed her and
dragged her inside. "Phyllis, I'm so
glad it's you!" Florence gasped.
"You have to help me!"

Phyllis told Florence that she
would be only too glad to help,
if she would only tell her why she
was so upset and why the house
looked like a horde of trolls had

been using it to play a game of five-a-side football.

"You silly banana!" Phyllis replied upon hearing Florence's predicament. "The answer's been under your nose all along!" And with that, she took her friend over to the bookshelf, and wiped her finger along it. "Fairy dust," she said, holding aloft a dust covered finger, "is simply the dust that gathers in the homes of all fairies!"

And so, if you should ever find yourself in a fairy's house, you'll know why the dusting never seems to get done!

Baron Beefburger

Written by Candy Wallace

A VERY LONG TIME AGO in a far off land, lived the evil Baron Beefburger. He had a twirly black moustache and a silly haircut that looked as though someone had put a pudding basin on his head and cut round it. He dressed in black and always had an evil sneer on his face.

The baron lived in a great castle and made his courtiers' lives an absolute misery. Not only was he always grumpy, but there was nothing he liked better than to hurl a custard pie in someone's face. The castle cooks worked day and night cooking the Baron's favourite beefburgers and an endless supply

of custard pies, while the castle laundry worked overtime cleaning all the custardy clothes.

In the castle lived the beautiful Princess Petunia and a knight called Sir Fightalot. Sir Fightalot was madly in love with the princess and she rather liked him too.

But the evil baron wanted the princess for himself. So poor Sir Fightalot received more than his fair share of custard pies and never had a clean suit of armour to wear.

One day, while Sir Fightalot was out jousting, the baron went to see the princess. When she saw him coming she put a box over her head quickly in case he had a custard pie with him.

"Come, come, my dear," said the baron in an oily voice. "I only want to talk to you." The princess took the box off her head and sat down with her chin in her hands looking glum. "What do you want?" she said, sulkily.

"I'm having a little dinner party tomorrow evening…" he said. 'Just for two…" and he put his face close to hers with a horrible smile. "I'd advise you to come, or you might find a custard pie in your bed…"

When Sir Fightalot returned and found out what the baron had been up to, he was hopping mad. Something had to be done.

He decided to go and see his wise
and tubby friend, Friar Tuckshop.

"We've got to do something
about him," said Sir Fightalot to his
friend the friar. "He's after the
princess and everyone in the castle
is sick and tired of being covered
in custard."

Friar Tuckshop looked
thoughtful. "There's only one
creature in the land more powerful
than the baron," he said finally.
"About 20 leagues away from here
lives a dragon in a cave on a
hillside. He's the only available
monster for miles. What's more, he's
not too keen on the baron. I
remember a couple of years ago the

baron sent the entire army to kill
the dragon and make him into an
umbrella stand for the Great Hall.
They didn't succeed, of course, but
it didn't make a very good
impression on the dragon. I think
he might help us."

The next morning, they set off
to find the dragon. Sir Fightalot's
knees were knocking the whole
way and Friar Tuckshop had to stop
every now and then for a restoring
snack. After some hours, walking
over hill and dale, they arrived at
the dragon's cave. It was set
halfway up a sheer rock face and
they could see the smoke from the
dragon's nostrils curling up into the

air outside the cave. Sir Fightalot looked at Friar Tuckshop and gulped.

"Are you sure he won't eat us?" he said.

"No, I'm not," Friar Tuckshop replied, "but it's too late to go back now!"

The two intrepid but trembling travellers climbed up to the mouth of the cave and peered in.

"Good afternoon," said the dragon. "Would you care for a cup of tea?"

Now it's a funny thing about dragons. People are very scared of them and run away. When they do go near one it's usually because

they want to kill it and take it back
to impress some princess or other,
which means that dragons get
rather lonely and fed up.

So the dragon was really pleased
to see the nervous, but friendly, Sir
Fightalot and Friar Tuckshop. They
found themselves being entertained
to a pot of tea and a plate of fairy
cakes. Very relieved they hadn't been
eaten after all, they explained

(in between mouthfuls of cake) about the troublesome baron's latest tricks. Together with the dragon (whose name was Humphrey) they devised a clever plan...

That night, the baron sat at one end of his huge dinner table in the Great Hall and poor Princess Petunia sat at the other end looking bored. The baron, with a napkin around his neck, was tucking into a plate of his favourite beefburgers smothered in tomato sauce. A pile of custard pies lay on the table ready for anyone who dared to interrupt his romantic candlelit dinner with the princess.

"Bah!" he spluttered, suddenly.

"These beefburgers are burnt!" He
turned in fury to a trembling
footman. "Bring the cook to me this
minute!" and he threw a custard pie
at the poor man as he sped out of
the door. Before you could say
"knife and fork", the door to the
Great Hall opened and in came —
Humphrey the dragon! He was
wearing a chef's hat and apron and
wielding a giant wooden spoon.
The baron was somewhat taken
aback, but managed to shout:

"These beefburgers are burnt
— you're fired!"

"No," replied the dragon. "You're
fired," and he breathed on the
baron's beefburgers. In seconds they

were reduced to smouldering cinders. The princess began to think this wasn't going to be such a bad evening after all. The baron, meanwhile, was speechless with terror and held his napkin over his face.

Into the room came Sir Fightalot and Friar Tuckshop.

"Our friend Humphrey here is going to be the new cook," said Sir Fightalot to the baron. "If you ever pester Princess Petunia again, or throw another custard pie, he'll burn your beefburgers to a cinder. Is that clear?"

Princess Petunia gazed at Sir Fightalot and sighed. What a hero!

The baron spluttered and

choked and went bright red and then deep purple. But he knew that he was beaten. What could a grumpy baron do against a big fire-breathing dragon?

After that, life was a lot easier at the castle.

Occasionally the baron just couldn't resist throwing a custard pie at someone and the dragon would burn his beefburgers that night. That would teach the baron a lesson — for a while, at least!

The princess was so impressed with brave Sir Fightalot that she married him.

Meanwhile, Humphrey the dragon stayed on as the castle cook

and was very happy. He loved cooking and, best of all, he wasn't lonely any more. He never did go back to his cave on the hillside. To thank him for taming the baron, the courtiers gave him a whole tower to himself and the run of the castle kitchen. Everyone agreed he made the best fairy cakes they had ever eaten and his fiery barbecues were the talk of the land. And if the baron fancied a custard pie — he had to make it himself!

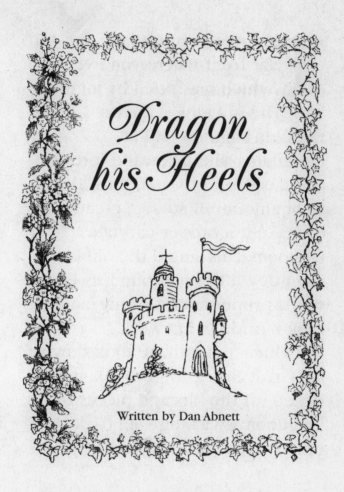

Dragon his Heels

Written by Dan Abnett

THERE ONCE was a land, not too far from where you live, which was ruled by an old king. The old king was very happy with his kingdom. It had mountains, and lakes, and forests, and a castle or two, and just the right amount of strange creatures to make it a proper fairytale kingdom. This suited the old king right down to the ground, as he was a proper fairytale king, and he took a pride in his work.

Once a month, he took down his Great Big Account Book and ticked off the bits and pieces of his kingdom. A wishing well (tick!), a unicorn (tick!), a fountain of youth (tick!), five fairies (tick!), a wicked witch (part time, Tuesdays and Thursdays only … tick!), four fierce lions (tick! tick! tick! tick!), a pack of wolves (tick!), a family of hill giants (tick!), two dragons (tick! and tick!), and a young prince/heir to the throne/son type thing (…er…tick!).

It was a busy time for the old king. Proper fairytale kingdoms don't just run themselves, you know. There was always something to fix. If it wasn't the wicked witch asking for an extra morning off, it was the wishing well wishing it was something else, like a public telephone box for instance.

That had taken some sorting out, I can tell you. It's all very well getting an operator who says, "your wish is my command," but you just try dialling up a casket of gold, a magic sword and a beautiful princess after six o'clock.

Anyway, one particular month, the old king sat with the Great Big Account Book across his knobbly old fairytale knees and noticed another thing that needed fixing.

"Oh, blow and tish!" said the

old king. "'Tish' is a very rude word in proper fairytale kingdoms, and only old kings are allowed to say it.

Already that morning he'd sorted out the go-slow at Tallboy and Sons Ltd, and helped elect a new leader for the wolf pack (the last one had left to go on a werewolfing course). But when he got to "two dragons" (tick!), he noticed that the account book now read, "three dragons."

He didn't, of course, tick that. Three dragons was far too many for a small fairytale kingdom, even if it was a proper one. Three dragons was excessive. Three dragons was... a dragon too many. It said so in his

How to Rule a Proper Fairytale Kingdom manual.

"We," said the old king, using the royal "we" (something else that only old kings are allowed to do), "will have to do something about this quick smart!"

The old king sent for his son. He was sure he had one of those young prince/heir to the throne/ son type of things. He'd ticked one off himself only the month before. Between you and me, the old king was a little concerned about the young prince. There were certain things a young prince had to do if he wanted to stay in the job, and this young prince hadn't shown signs of doing any of them. "Well, that's about to change," said the old king to himself.

The young prince came when called, and smiled at the old king in a friendly way.

"I want you to seek out a dragon and kill it," said the old king.

"Pardon, Dad?" the young prince said. "I want you to seek out a dragon and kill it," repeated the old king. "We've got far too many, and that's what young princes do. And don't call me 'Dad.' It's undignified. Call me your Highness."

"Okay," said the young prince, a little confused. "About this dragon … why have I got to kill it?"

"We've got too many of them. And it says here in my manual that young princes are supposed to seek out and dispose of any excess dragons. It's part of their job."

So off went the young prince. He wasn't too happy about it. He'd never killed anything in his young and princely life, and he wasn't really sure he wanted to.

But he put on his silver armour, collected his lance and his white charger, and off he went. He looked terrific, just like a young prince should do. Even the wicked witch approved (it was, mind you, her day off).

After a long journey, the young

prince arrived at the place on his map marked 'Here Be Dragons.' He got down from his white charger and walked towards a cave.

"Hello? Dragons? Are you home?" he called into the cave.

"Hold on," said a voice. "I'll be right out."

After a moment, a dragon came out of the cave. It wasn't a very big dragon at all, and the young prince

was quite disappointed (and rather pleased at the same time). The dragon was no taller than the prince, but it was a real dragon. It had a mouthful of long fangs, a tail that ended in a little arrowhead spike, a coat of the most splendid green scales, and a pair of tiny wings. When it spoke, little flames crackled along its forked tongue.

"And you are?" asked the small dragon.

"The young prince," said the young prince.

"Pleased to meet you. I'm the small dragon," said the small dragon. They shook hands, and the small dragon offered the young prince a glass of lemonade., which was thoughtful of him, as the young prince had ridden a fair distance and was thirsty. They sat and sipped their lemonade. The young prince was particularly impressed by the way the small dragon stuck out his littlest claw as he held the glass. A sign of polite breeding, his father would have said.

"So what can I do for you, Young Prince?" asked the small dragon. "I'm afraid my mum and dad, the big dragons, are out at the moment. Princesses to menace, villages to burn with their flaming breath … you know how it is."

"Well, you see, the thing is …"

began the young prince. "Actually, I've got to find a dragon and kill it. Dad says I must."

"Oh!" said the small dragon.

"Sorry," said the young prince.

"Must you?" said the small dragon.

"'Fraid so," said the young prince.

"I wouldn't want you to disobey your dad, of course, but is there any way we could skip the actual 'killing a dragon' bit?" asked the small dragon.

"I don't know," said the young prince, thoughtfully. "It depends. Can you play hide and seek?"

When the young prince got

home, the old king had the Great Big Account Book open on his famously knobbly knees.

"Dragons?" he asked, sternly.

"Two," said the young prince.

"Tick! Well done! Young prince/heir to the throne/son type of things who do what they're asked to do?" asked the old king.

"One. Right here," said the young prince.

"Tick!" said the old king happily, ticking.

"You'd better add a new bit to your accounts, though, your Highness," said the young prince after a pause.

"And what would that be?"

asked the old king, starting a new page and reaching for his ruler.

"Friends of the young prince/heir to the throne/son type of thing," said the young prince.

"How many?" asked the old king.

"One," said the prince, smiling.

"Made a friend, did you?" asked the old king, closing the Great Big Account Book and looking up with a smile.

"Yes," said the young prince. "One who's much better at hiding than I am at seeking."

And from that day on, there have been the right number of ticks in the old king's book.

Desmond the Dragon

Written by Amber Hunt

YOUNG DESMOND THE DRAGON was by now absolutely, utterly, and almost nearly sure that he wasn't a dragon. Oh, he was a respectable size, and growing all the time, and he was covered from ears to tail with very tough and very green scales. He had a forked tongue, just like all his friends, and four sets of fine claws as well as a good loud dragon-type roar. Desmond had to admit that he did look a lot like his mum and dad, but, despite all this, Desmond was still worried that he might not be a real dragon.

Each morning he looked in the mirror, twisting around to examine

his back and each morning he saw
— nothing. Dragons had wings,
didn't they? If he was a dragon,
where were his wings?

Then, after he had looked in
the mirror, Desmond would go
outside the cave into the garden
and breathe out hard. Nothing.
Dragons breathed fire, didn't they?
If he was a dragon, where was
his fire?

Desmond decided that if he
wasn't a dragon, and by now he
was almost and very nearly sure he
wasn't, then he must be — a
dinosaur!

He spent hours gazing at his
books on dinosaurs, trying to work

out which dinosaur he looked most like, but he always came to the same conclusion — he didn't look like any of them.

Desmond was very confused. His mum and dad didn't seem to notice that he wasn't a dragon, but then perhaps when they asked him to light the fire, they didn't realise that he couldn't just breathe on it the way they did — oh no, he had to light the fire by rubbing two sticks together. And maybe they didn't realise that the reason he left the house very early to go to school was because he couldn't fly there, and it took a long time to walk.

Desmond liked going to dragon

school. He liked his teachers and he had lots of friends, none of whom seemed to notice that he wasn't really a dragon. But then you weren't allowed to fly during school, so perhaps that was why they hadn't realised. The fact that he couldn't breathe fire wasn't a problem either; all dragons, upon

arriving at school, had to drink a gallon of water. This prevented young dragons, who weren't yet properly fire-trained, from acciden-tally breathing out flames and setting fire to the school. So Desmond's secret was safe, for now.

Then one day Desmond woke up with a fang-ache. At first he wasn't sure what it was. He thought perhaps his head was lying on something sharp, but when he sat up the pain went with him and it followed him out of bed and all the way over to the mirror.

He looked in the mirror and didn't see himself looking back. Well, not the himself he was used to seeing. The dragon, or possibly not dragon, he was looking at, had a huge swelling on the side of its face.

Desmond rushed downstairs to his mum., "Mum," he mumbled, "look at my face. It has gone all lumpy and bumpy."

Desmond's mum looked at his face and, trying not to laugh, said, "Oh dear, I think you have been eating too many chocolate-covered bones. We'd better go and see Morris the Magician. He's a wonderful fangtist, amongst other things." She winked at Desmond's dad, and while Desmond went to get his hat, said to him, "I think it's time to get a couple of other things

sorted out too while we're there, don't you, dear?"

So off they went to see Morris. "It's such a nice day," said Mrs Dragon, with a knowing smile. "I think we'll walk." And they did, much to Desmond's relief. Desmond sat in Morris the Magician's special chair and waited, while his mum talked to Morris outside.

He was trying to be brave and fearless, as he knew a good dragon should be, but his knees kept knocking together at the thought of what Morris might do. Then Morris came in and sat on a stool next to him and asked Desmond to open his mouth wide.

"This won't hurt," he said.

"Uh, huh, uh, huh, mmm," muttered Morris. "Ah yes, yes, I have it, I can see the problem." He smiled at Desmond. "You have a bone caught behind one of your fangs and it's pressing into the gum. The bone is stuck quite fast which is why your fang brush couldn't get it out. You do brush your fangs, don't you, Desmond?" asked Morris, sternly.

"Eth, I oo," said Desmond, which was all he could manage with his mouth open, "Effery hay."

"Good. Now," explained Morris, "I am going to use a little bit of magic, so that when I take the bone out it won't hurt. Then you can go home, and hopefully all your worries will be over." Saying that, he waved his wand, mumbled some magic words, and cast a spell over Desmond.

Some time later, Desmond opened his eyes. Looking around him, he slowly remembered where he was. Pleased to discover the bone gone he breathed a great sigh of relief, and a huge ball of flames came shooting out! Fortunately, he didn't burn anything.

"Look, look," he shouted. "See, I am a dragon. I can breathe fire!" and he beamed at his mum and Morris.

Morris smiled a secret magician's smile and exchanged a knowing look with Mrs Dragon.

"Of course you can," he said. "We always knew you would when the time was right. You can't hurry these things you know. I think you will find that you can unfold your wings now as well."

Desmond looked at Morris mystified. Mrs Dragon thanked the magician and she and Desmond went outside. Then, without thinking, Desmond unfurled his tightly folded wings — they had been there all along. He nearly fell over with surprise. Desmond's mum smiled.

"I think you're ready to try flying now. Perhaps we can practice on the way home."

Excitedly, Desmond waved goodbye to Morris, who, still smiling a secret magician's smile, was watching from his cave window.

Desmond opened his wings and wobbled into the air.

Then, his confidence growing, he soared up into the sky and flew round a few times — looking and feeling like the noble dragon he was.

And finally, he flew home for tea with his mum.

A Dream Come True

Written by Geoff Cowan

WHAT HAS huge claws and teeth, a long scaly body and tail, breathes fire and likes ice-cream? Answer: a dragon with a problem!

And that's why Smoky was fed-up. Now you may be forgiven for thinking dragons are horrible, fearsome, fiery creatures who do no good to anyone. But you'd be wrong. At least, you would be in the case of Smoky and all the other dragons who lived on the small, volcanic island of Dragonia.

It was the perfect place to be; for a dragon, that is. The volcano huffed and puffed gently all day, like the dragons, who were rather a lazy lot. They lay beneath its smouldering slopes, enjoying the warm air and dozing peacefully; until they were hungry. Then they had big helpings of delicious home-made dishes, such as pumpkin pie and fruit flan, all heated in a fiery flash, of course!

Home-made? Yes. Not by the dragons but by the grateful townsfolk of Tastyville, across the water. For longer than anyone could remember, the dragons had been model neighbours. They could always be depended on in times of trouble, which is why the Dragon Gong hung in the town square to be sounded in emergencies. Then the dragons would stir themselves with surprising speed, unfold their leathery wings and fly to Tastyville to offer help faster than you could say, "dragon's breath"!

Whether it was to drive away invaders long ago, or in more recent times, just to fire up the blacksmith's forge on a wet morning, it didn't matter. The dragons would have a go at anything. They were very handy do-gooders to know. In return, the

people of Tastyville fed them with all sorts of tasty treats. Apart from one important exception — ice-cream. The fame of the Tastyville Ice-Cream Factory knew no limits, save the shores of Dragonia. After all, how could such a fire-spouting bunch of dragons possibly eat ice-cold ice-cream? There would be meltdown the moment their burning breath settled on it.

Which is why Smoky dreamt of nothing else; ice-cream was the only food he couldn't have, which made him want it all the more. That and the fact that he was the only dragon ever to have eaten any!

What have dragons and

elephants in common? Answer: long memories. After all, people say that elephants never forget and neither had Smoky. He had hardly hatched from his shell on that distant day when his mum returned from good-deed-doing in Tastyville with a tub of ice-cream for him.

Smoky had been too tiny then to breathe fire. So he'd lapped up the scrummy, fabulous, frozen delight, which now, sadly, he could only dream about.

Then one winter something happened that would make Smoky's dreams come true. It became known as the Coldest Winter. Tastyville shivered beneath the thickest snow anyone had ever known. Everything froze, even the sea in the harbour. So the mayor went to sound the Dragon Gong but couldn't find it under a snowdrift. Luckily, Smoky was practising some stunt-flying nearby. He saw the mayor waving frantically and went to find out what was wrong.

"If the sea-ice doesn't melt, ships won't get through with food for the town," explained the mayor.

"No food for Tastyville means none for us, either," thought Smoky, gloomily. "We've tried dropping rocks on the ice but it won't even crack!" the mayor went on. "You must help us!"

"Stay cool," replied Smoky, blushing as he realised that wasn't the best thing to say. He quickly added, "I mean, don't get steamed up!" He decided that wasn't right either and became quite tongue-tied. But the mayor knew Smoky had something helpful in mind and watched the dragon wing its way back to Dragonia.

"I'll be back!" roared Smoky, through a cloud of scorching flame.

When he returned, he was not alone. The wintry sky was filled with beating wings. Not a single dragon stayed behind on Dragonia. Wrapping up warmly, the excited townsfolk hurried to the harbour to watch in wonder as the fiery flock hovered over the frozen sea.

"If anyone can melt the sea-ice, we're hot favourites!" bellowed Smoky.

Every dragon began to blast the ice with burning breath. So great was the heat that a golden red glow filled the sky. The snow over Tastyville dripped away and the townsfolk bathed in the warmth.

But the ice didn't melt; not at first. It was so thick, it stubbornly withstood the flame-throwing dragons.

"Breathe harder," rasped Smoky, a hot dryness in his throat.

More flames, more roaring, raging fire until, at last, less ice. First, the surface turned to water. Then the rest seemed to give up and melt all of a sudden. The harbour was open at last. Even as the thankful people of Tastyville cheered, a ship sailed closer, bringing much-needed fresh food.

Everyone jumped up and down, and danced and sang for joy. Everyone, that is, except for Smoky. He lay wearily at the harbourside and seemed unable to move.

"What's wrong?" asked the worried mayor. "Are you ill? Do you need a doctor?"

"No, just … ice-cream!"

whispered Smoky, his eyes half-closed.

"Ice-cream?!" gasped the mayor. "But what use is that to a dragon?"

All the same, a big tub of it was

fetched from the factory and placed near Smoky. Everyone waited anxiously as he slowly scooped some up on the tip of his tongue.

"Amazing! It hasn't melted!" cried the mayor. "I don't understand!"

Smoky smiled blissfully as he swallowed the cold, creamy mix. It was the most delicious thing he had ever tasted. Slipping easily down his dry throat, it soothed the soreness from so much fire.

"It's simple," he said quietly. "I am so puffed out, that I'm not breathing hard enough to melt the ice-cream. If I just remember to breathe very gently indeed, I can eat all I want!"

Since then, Smoky has flown to the ice-cream factory once a week for a king-sized cornet or two, and only the odd one ever melts before it reaches his mouth!

So now what has huge claws and teeth, a long scaly body and tail, breathes fire and eats ice-cream? Answer: one very happy dragon!

Wonderwhiskers

Written by Geoff Cowan

DOWN AMONG the plants and shrubs, in many a garden, you may come across a little painted stone figure with a bushy white beard and red, pointed hat. Often as not, he's sitting on a toadstool or fishing with a tiny rod.

These little folk are, of course, garden gnomes. If you've seen one, then you'll know what a real gnome looks like.

Well, Wonderwhiskers was no different, except for his beard. It was the thickest, strongest and longest you could imagine. In fact, it was so long that Wonderwhiskers had to part it down the middle and, with the help of other gnomes, roll

it up into two bundles which he carried on his back.

Any sensible gnome would have cut such a beard and, in the early days, Wonderwhiskers had tried to. But by next day, it had always grown longer than before.

"Amazing!" he'd gasp, as he stared at his beard in the mirror. So he decided he'd just have to live with it.

Besides, Wonderwhiskers was very proud of his beard. It had made him famous! The other gnomes treated him with the greatest respect, and would do anything he asked them. There wasn't a gnome in the land who hadn't invited him home for a slap-up meal. Oh, yes!

Wonderwhiskers was definitely a V.I.G., a Very Important Gnome. But it had not always been like that...

There was a time when Wonderwhiskers had been just your average common-or-garden gnome, by the name of Norman. He had lived in a snug underground home beneath an old storm-struck tree, deep in the heart of the forest. Norman and his gnome neighbours would go in search of tiny treasures to decorate their home, such as shiny pebbles, a lucky four-leaved clover or even a fluffy feather, dropped by one of their bird friends.

That, however, was before Norman's beard had begun to grow and grow. Before long it became a bit of a nuisance. The end would blow into Norman's face so that he couldn't see where he was going. Once, Norman had walked straight into his friend Tiggletum who dropped a sackful of forest treasures on his toe. Even after Norman began to roll up his beard, it sometimes came loose and dragged along the ground, like the time when his cousin Lightstep tripped on it and went flying into a puddle.

Yet, every night before he went to bed, Norman always washed and brushed his beard before measuring it to see just how much longer it had grown. Such a big, bushy beard made him feel special.

"The bigger his beard, the bigger Norman's head!" others began to utter with just a teensy-weensy hint of jealousy as word spread of his incredible beard, and visitors came from far and wide to see it.

Then, one day, some unbelievable news caused the gnomes to chatter excitedly.

"King Cracklecorn's coming! Imagine! The King of the Gnomes visiting us!" cried Norman's neighbours.

"He must have heard about my beard, too," said Norman proudly.

"Don't flatter yourself," replied Tiggletum. "He's coming because I wrote to him!"

"You what?!" gasped Norman.

"Didn't I tell you?" continued Tiggletum, looking oh-so-smug. "I found the rarest treasure of all. The king's sure to reward me!"

"What is it, this treasure?" asked Norman.

"It's the place where the rainbow ends," announced Tiggletum. "Every gnome knows it's a magical place, where you'll find a pot of gold!"

"Why didn't you bring the gold back with you?" asked another gnome, called Bizzybonce.

Tiggletum shuffled his feet and looked awkward. "Well, I think I've found the rainbow's end," he explained. "One sunny afternoon last week I went out for a walk, but it began to rain. A rainbow appeared. I saw one end dip towards a clearing. I ran all the way there but, by the time I arrived, the rain had stopped so the rainbow

vanished. But I should be able to find the spot again!"

"I hope so!" frowned Lightfoot. "Fancy inviting the king without being sure!"

It was too late for Tiggletum to start worrying now. Before they knew it the king was on the doorstep and they all set off to find the rainbow's end. By the time they had covered half the forest and walked in circles for a few hours,

everyone was feeling grumpy,
especially the king.

To make matters worse, it
began to rain. No sun, mind you;
just rain, rain and more rain. As they
hurried back to their homes, they
decided to take the short cut
beside the brook. But it had
swollen to a fast-flowing stream and
that's when the King had an
accident. He slipped, fell in and was
nearly washed away.

"Someone fetch a rope!" yelled
Tiggletum, as King Cracklecorn
clung to a piece of driftwood that,
for a lucky moment, had jammed
between two rocks amid the rapids.

"We don't have a rope! We don't

have anything that can save him!" cried Bizzybonce.

"Oh, yes we have!" replied Norman. He unrolled his beard which he'd kept neatly behind his back as usual. Next moment, he threw the end to the king who managed to grasp it.

"Hold on, your Majesty!" called Norman. Turning to the others, he said, "Hurry! Help me pull him towards us!"

Inch by inch, through the surging water, the King of the Gnomes was pulled closer. Norman closed his eyes, bit his lip and never uttered a sound, although it must have been very painful. After all, imagine how hard his beard was being tugged! Ouch!

But, at last, helping hands lifted the weary king clear and he sat puffing on the riverbank. Soaked but safe, he turned to Norman.

"I hereby name you Wonderwhiskers," he said thankfully, "and grant you the title of S.M.I.G!"

"Second Most Important Gnome," whispered Tiggletum to the others in amazement. "That means only the king is more important than Norman, I mean Wonderwhiskers, now!"

They all thought he had been incredibly brave and clever. As they went to congratulate him, they slipped on his dripping beard, toppled into each other and landed in a happy heap. Everyone laughed, including the king.

And from that day on, the invitations poured through Wonderwhiskers' letterbox. He spent his time enjoying one visit after another, to tell his famous story or show off his fabulous beard. His admiring hosts did everything they could to make such a noble gnome feel comfortable.

As Wonderwhiskers often joked to himself, it was just like home from home ... or gnome from gnome!

Ned the Gnome

Written by Amber Hunt

NED THE GNOME spent the morning sticking his feet into icky sticky mud puddles and breathing deeply the horrible smell that accompanies icky sticky mud. He tried to tell himself he loved the mud and adored the smell, but he didn't, not really ... not even a little bit.

Eventually, feeling quite down in the dumps, Ned went and sat on the top of a little hill, wondering what he was going to do.

"Excuse me," said a voice behind him, "but why don't you smell?"

"What?" said Ned, startled. "Why should I smell?"

"I asked a question first," replied the voice, "and you can't answer a question with a question. It's rude. But then you're a gnome, so I suppose rudeness is all that can be expected from you ... so why don't you smell then?" Ned turned to see a rabbit peeking its head out of a burrow behind him.

"Well, that's the problem," said Ned. "Not that it's any of your business, but I don't like dirt and mud and I hate being rude to people."

"I see," scoffed the rabbit. "A clean, polite gnome. I suppose you expect me to believe that, do you? All gnomes are rude, dirty and smell horrible." The rabbit sniffed loudly. "I don't like gnomes, never have and never shall."

"Oh," said the gnome. "Well, what makes you think rabbits are so perfect, always digging holes for us little folk to fall down?" and so saying, he turned his back on the rabbit.

"Do you really like being clean?" ventured the rabbit, after a while. "Doesn't that make life a bit difficult with the other gnomes?"

"Of course it does," replied Ned. "I've been trying all morning to like mud and enjoy the smell. Yesterday I even practised being

rude, but it's no good," he sighed. "All the other gnomes laugh at me, you know."

The gnome and the rabbit sat for a while side by side, deep in thought.

"Got it," said the rabbit suddenly. "I think I know where there might be some clean gnomes, although I've only seen them from a distance," she admitted, "so I don't know about the politeness bit."

"Really? Where? Please tell me." The gnome jumped up.

"I'll do better than that, I'll show you. Follow me!" And the rabbit hopped off with Ned following closely behind.

Soon they arrived at the top of a steep hill. Climbing down, they came to a house, the sort that humans live in. Surrounding the house was a garden and in the garden was a large pond. Sitting round the pond were several very clean gnomes.

"Ooh, look at them," said Ned in awe. He left the rabbit nibbling plants and flowers in the garden and went to talk to the gnomes.

"Hello, I'm Ned," he said to a gnome who was sitting holding a tiny fishing rod.

"Sshh," hissed the gnome. "We don't talk during the day, we only talk at night." And with that he sat staring ahead, refusing to say another word.

Going back to the rabbit, Ned explained: "They only talk at night, so I think I'll wait and talk to them then."

"Right-oh," said the rabbit, who had taken quite a liking to Ned. "I'll pop back later and see how you're getting on."

Ned found a large bush near the pond. He wriggled into the centre of it, made himself comfortable and fell asleep.

Later, when the stars were out, Ned woke up. Remembering where he was, he crawled excitedly out of the bush and went up to the gnome he'd spoken to earlier.

"Hello," he said. "My name is Ned."

"Sshh," whispered the gnome, "you'll frighten the fish."

"Can I whisper to you?" whispered Ned.

"If you must," replied the gnome.

In hushed tones Ned explained

his problem and said that if they were all nice, clean, polite gnomes, then he would like to join them please. The gnome thought for a while.

"O.K.," he said eventually. "My name's Grunt. Go and sit over there," and he pointed to a space between two other gnomes.

Ned did as he was told.

"Hello," said Ned to the gnome on his left. "My name is Ned. What's yours?"

"Sshh," said the gnome. "We aren't allowed to talk much in case we disturb the fish, or worse still, wake up the humans."

Ned sat quietly for a while,

then, feeling stiff, he got up to stretch his legs.

"Sit still," hissed a voice to his right. "We aren't allowed to move, we might..."

"Disturb the fish," finished Ned. "Yes, I thought as much. Don't you get bored?"

"Of course we don't," whispered the gnome. "We've trained ourselves not to."

Later, the wind started to blow and one of the gnomes fell over, but no one went to help him.

"Why doesn't he get up? Is he hurt?" Ned asked the gnome next to him, in surprise.

"No," came the reply. "He's made

of plastic, as are some of the others. They belong to the humans."

Ned looked round and thought to himself, "I can't tell the difference."

"Do you live like this all the time?" he asked the gnome to his right.

"Of course. It is our job to watch over the fish. We have to protect them."

Ned sat for a while longer. At the far end of the garden he could see that his friend the rabbit had returned. Quietly he left the pond and went over to her.

"I have never been so bored in all my life," he told the rabbit.

"My friends might be rude and dirty, and they might smell a bit, but at least they're not boring."

"Time to go home, I think," said the rabbit.

When Ned finally arrived home, everybody made a huge fuss

of him. He'd been greatly missed. He told the other gnomes about his adventures and they were all very upset that he had nearly left them and so it was decided that they should make a pact.

It was agreed that no gnome would mind if Ned was clean, sweet smelling and polite, as long as Ned did not mind that the others were sometimes rude, almost always dirty, or that they smelled a bit. After that Ned was never ever tempted to leave his gnome home again, although he did sometimes go for long walks with his special friend the rabbit.

Gnome Improvements

Written by Claire Steeden

IN A SMALL garden centre, in a town not far from here, lived a gnome called George. At night, when it was dark and everyone had gone home, George and the rest of his gnome friends played on the swings and slides there and even swam in the pond. They all had lots of fun but were careful that nobody saw them move, hurrying back to their positions before it got light.

One morning, George overheard Sam, the owner, talking to Sarah, who worked there part-time.

"The garden gnomes don't seem to be selling well this year. I don't understand it, they've always been so popular," said Sam.

"Maybe they're too expensive. Why don't we put them on sale?" replied Sarah.

"That's a good idea. Could you paint a sign saying 'All gnomes half price'?" asked Sam.

"O.K. I'll do it this afternoon," said Sarah.

George was listening nearby. He felt worried all day, and that night he called a meeting to tell the others what he had overheard.

"That's terrible," cried Grace. "If we all get sold to different people we'll never see each other again."

"I don't want to be sold. I want to stay here with all of you," sobbed Gloria. "What are we going to do?"

asked Gilbert. They all stood there thinking hard.

"We could run away," suggested Gladys.

"But where would we go? We've never been outside the garden centre," said Gerald. "Don't worry," said George. "I think I've got a good idea."

George had watched while Sarah had painted the sale sign. She had used paints and brushes kept in one of the garden sheds.

"Come with me and I'll tell you my plan," said George.

All the gnomes followed George to the shed. "Once we are on sale tomorrow lots of people will want to buy us. They like plain red and white gnomes in their gardens. But if we paint each other in lots of bright colours and patterns we'll look so awful that nobody will want us," explained George.

"That's a brilliant idea," cried Gladys, and all the others agreed. They could hardly wait to get started.

They pulled the shed door open and went inside. George climbed up an old wooden ladder and switched the light on.

One by one they opened the tins of paint. Throughout the night they had great fun painting each other in the brightest colours and most outrageous patterns they could think of. George had an orange hat with purple spots, lime green hair, a red and yellow striped jacket, blue trousers with silver stars and the brightest pair of pink boots you have ever seen! The rest of the gnomes looked just as dreadful. As they stood looking at each other, they started to laugh.

"We look awful," cried Grace.

"Nobody will want us in their garden," chuckled Gloria.

"I think we all look marvellous," said Gladys. "Let's just hope nobody else does!"

It was daylight when they

finished clearing up — nearly time for Sam and Sarah to arrive for work. They just had time to get to their places and stand still before Sam and Sarah walked through the gate.

Sam took one look at the gnomes and let out a shriek.

"Aarghh, what's happened to the gnomes? We'll never sell them looking like that!"

George winked at the others.

"Some kids must have got in last night and mucked about. But look at the colours they've used! Even at half price nobody will buy them," said Sarah. "Come on, let's have a cup of tea."

All day long the customers remarked on how funny the gnomes looked.

"What a sight. I wouldn't have one in my garden if they were giving them away," said one man.

Then just before closing time an old lady came through the gate.

"Oh my," she cried when she saw the gnomes. "How wonderful! I've got a couple of gnomes in my garden but none as splendid as these."

"You mean you like them, madam?" asked Sam.

"Like them? I love them," she replied. "But which one shall I choose?"

On hearing this all the gnomes started to panic. Which one would she buy and take away with her?

"I can't decide," she sighed. "They're all so funny."

"They're half price in our sale, madam," said Sam. "Maybe you'd like more than one."

"What a splendid idea," she

said. "In fact, I'll take them all. I can't do much gardening any more so I haven't got many flowers. These gnomes will add a splash of colour and make the garden look more cheerful."

"All of them? Are you sure?" asked Sam.

"Quite sure. It'll be money well spent," replied the lady. Sam took the lady's address so that they could be delivered. Sarah packed them into a big box and put them into the van.

On the way, George whispered to the others, "I don't want to leave the garden centre, but at least we're all together."

When they arrived Sarah carried the box to the front door and rang the bell.

"Oh good. I was hoping you'd be here before dark. I can't wait to put them in the garden," said the old lady.

Sarah carried them through to the back garden. When she had gone the lady carefully unpacked them one by one.

When they were all unwrapped she said, "My name is Daisy. Welcome to my home. It won't be as lonely now with all of you to talk to. It's just a shame you can't talk back."

Daisy put the gnomes around

her lovely little garden. When she had finished she stood back to look at them. "My you are colourful. You certainly brighten up my garden."

As it was getting dark, Daisy went inside and drew the curtains. After a while the gnomes started to whisper to each other.

"What a pretty garden," said Gilbert.

"There's a pond and a swing,"

said George. "It's probably for her grandchildren."

The other gnomes in the garden introduced themselves, and soon they were all chatting like old friends.

"I think we're going to be very happy living here," said Gladys, smiling.

When Daisy's friends saw the gnomes they wanted some too, so Sarah started to paint the new gnomes at the garden centre. They sold so quickly she could not paint them fast enough. Sam was pleased as business had never been so good, and it was all because of the friendly gnomes who wanted to stay together.

Gnome Sweet Gnome

Written by Dan Abnett

JUST WEST of the snow-capped Candlemass Mountains, at the point where the Great West Road crosses the Green River, you'll find a little pottery business run by a family of gnomes called the Slightlys. These gnomes are kind, generous little people, no taller than a chair leg. They never shout or say rude words or pull hair, they never leave things in a mess and they never have a bad word to say about anyone.

Gnomes are great craftsmen, and the Slightlys are no exception. They have owned the little pottery for years making the finest teapots, bowls, dishes and jugs you'll ever see. Travellers often stop and buy something from the Slightlys' shop. Each item of Gnomeware comes packed in straw in a little wooden box with a label that reads "Slightly Gnome-made".

Mr Slightly is the master potter, and spends all day in the

workshop, making the Gnomeware on his potter's wheel. His sister, Everso Slightly, is in charge of the kiln, where she bakes the soft pottery until it's hard. Mrs Slightly and her daughter, Very, paint lovely patterns on the Gnomeware, and glaze them shiny and bright, and Grandma and Grandpa Slightly run the shop.

Then of course, there's young Od. He's Mr Slightly's son, and a fine young figure of a gnome.

It had always been assumed that Od Slightly would follow in the family footsteps and one day become the master potter himself. Every day, he studied as an apprentice in the workshop. Trouble was, try as he might, Od wasn't very keen on pot-making. He just didn't have his father's patience, or his steady hand. Od's dishes always looked a little wobbly. The handles fell off his jugs, the lids never fitted his bowls, and he was forever getting confused and putting two spouts on his teapots. More than once, he'd lost control of the potter's wheel completely, and sent wet, floppy clay splatting all over the nice clean workshop.

Whenever things went wrong, Od's father would stand with his hands on his hips, shaking his head sadly. Mrs Slightly would say, "There, there, Od," and go and fetch the dustpan and mop.

Very Slightly, who could paint patterns on the Gnomeware every bit as well as her mum, would snigger at her brother in a very superior way.

All day long, Od dreamed fantastic dreams of high adventure and peril. He was Od the Pirate Gnome, Od the Jungle Explorer, Od the Racing Car Driver, Od the Test Pilot. ...He had a stack of old *Ideal Gnome* magazines, which were full of articles about high fliers in the gnome world. Film star gnomes and secret agent gnomes and million pound-transfer footballer gnomes called Gnozza. "One day. . ." he'd say to himself, as he sponged clay-blobs off the workshop wall, ". ..one day I'll pack my things, leave this miserable, boring, clay-filled life and go off to seek my fortune. I'll become Very Famous Gnome Celebrity Od Slightly and send exciting postcards home to mum and dad. Just let Very snigger at me then." As an afterthought, he added to himself, "I'll probably have to change my name, though, if I'm going to be a Very Famous Gnome Celebrity. Something like Brad Slightly or Rock Slightly would sound more cool."

One particular morning, Od's latest edition of *Ideal Gnome* magazine arrived in the post. In the classified section was an advert that quite took Od's breath away.

"Good-looking young gnomes required for ornamental duties. Apply to the Royal Palace of King Barnabus II."

When Mr Slightly got up for work, he couldn't find Od anywhere. He checked the house and the workshop, but Od was nowhere to be found. Then Aunt Everso found a note pinned to the kiln.

"Gone to seek fortune. Have taken clean underwear. Will write soon." It was signed, "Od."

"Oh dear me..." murmured Mrs Slightly.

It took Od three days to reach the palace of King Barnabus II. He was tired and weary by the time he arrived at the gates. If it hadn't been for the lift he'd got for the last ten miles on the back of an ox cart, he was sure he'd never have made it.

The palace was huge, even by gnome standards. Little Od looked around in awe. Big people marched about the place being important. Trumpets blasted out fanfares that made him jump out of his shoes. He had to scurry out of the way of enormous, stomping soldiers, and horses on parade. Even the dwarf footmen looked down on him. Eventually he found his way to the Lord Chamberlain's office and knocked nervously at the door.

"Come in," boomed a deep voice from inside. The chamberlain peered down at him over the top of his glasses with a scornful sneer, and dabbed his pen in the inkpot. "Name?"

"Erm. . . Shane Slightly," said Od, in a rather shaky voice. He was trembling so hard that his knees knocked together.

"Slightly... hmmm," said the chamberlain, writing it down in a big book. "And you're here for the gnome job?"

"The ornamental one, that's right, sir," said Od with a friendly grin. The chamberlain didn't smile back. Od didn't really know what the job was about, but he reckoned that if it was ornamental, it probably meant he was going to be a gnome model. Maybe he'd be paid millions and appear on the cover of glamorous fashion magazines.

"Follow me," said the chamberlain, and led him through the huge palace gardens and down to the lake. He handed Od a small fishing rod.

"Sit there," he said, pointing to a rock on the lake edge, "and pretend to fish."

"Is that all?" asked Od.

"You'll work from sunrise until sunset, unless there's an evening garden party, in which case you work overtime. On no account are you to move, wander about or do anything except look ornamental." The chamberlain stomped off and left Od to it. Od sat down on the

rock, feeling rather uneasy. Two hours later, he still felt uneasy, but now he felt hot and uncomfortable too. He was bored. His neck was stiff, and there was an annoying fly buzzing around his ear. The Chamberlain came back to check on him.

"Very good, but try smiling too," he said.

"What do I do when I've finished this?" asked Od.

"What do you mean, 'finish'," replied the Chamberlain, looking taken aback. "This is what you're paid to do. You're an ornamental garden gnome."

Od was halfway home, trudging along the Great West Road, when he met Grandpa Slightly coming the other way.

"Thought I might find you out here, young Od," said Grandpa. They fell into step, heading back towards the Candlemass Mountains, where the sun was just setting.

"You know, more than anything else, I want to make a big teapot." said Od. "I've really got the urge."

"That's the spirit," said Grandpa.

Od thought a while, then said, "I've decided, Grandpa. Wherever you go, there's really no place like gnome."

Bulky the Giant

Written by Geoff Cowan

As GIANTS GO, Bulky was okay. He was what you might call a gentle giant. He was always polite to the local villagers. He did his very best not to upset them, which, being huge, wasn't easy.

Take Bulky's feet, for instance. His shoes seemed like boats to the villagers. Even if Bulky tiptoed past their homes, he still made the ground tremble. The startled folk fell out of bed, kitchen crockery rattled and furniture bounced about.

The villagers complained to Bulky. They only dared to because he was so nice and kind. He even said sorry and promised to creep around more carefully than before.

"I should think so," said the villagers, impatiently.

Then there was his sneezing. Now everyone sneezes from time to time, and giants are no different. But when Bulky sneezed he sent such a blast of air howling across the valley, the villagers had to rush indoors for fear of being blown away!

They complained to Bulky about that as well. The giant promised he would sneeze into his hanky, which, after all, is only the polite thing to do. But sometimes a sneeze came upon him all of a sudden, before he could do anything about it.

One complaint followed another. Eventually the villagers decided life would be much more comfortable without a giant living on their doorstep. So they sent for Spellbound the Wizard and asked him if he could shrink Bulky down to normal human size.

Bulky agreed to the plan at once, proving what a big-hearted giant he was!

"Abracadabra, pots, pans and sink,
A wave of my wand will make
Bulky shrink!"

As Spellbound chanted the rhyme he gave his wand a few

extra waves for luck. Sometimes, his spells needed it!

All at once, a silvery mist appeared, hiding Bulky from sight. When it cleared, the delighted villagers saw that Bulky was just the same size as them!

For a while everyone lived peacefully. Bulky moved in with a kind family who looked after him very well, and he began to enjoy life at his new size.

Now life's full of little surprises but the surprise that arrived from beyond the mountains surrounding the villagers' valley was big as in giant; the walking, talking type, just like Bulky used to be!

Heavyhand was short-tempered and always wanted to get his own way. The villagers didn't know this at first. But they soon found out. When Heavyhand lay down for snooze in a lush, green meadow, sending sheep scattering, the villagers complained, just as they had to Bulky.

But Heavyhand roared angrily at them and warned that if he wasn't left in peace, he would flatten every home in the village! Then he banged his fist mightily on the ground. The frightened villagers jumped into the air, and scattered in all directions.

"Clear off!" he bellowed. "I like

this valley and I'm here to stay!"
From that day on, Heavyhand
stomped about wherever he
pleased, flattening crops, and
knocking down trees. When he lay
down for a rest, he always slipped
off his boots and used them as a
pillow. He had horribly smelly feet,
and the rotten pong wafted

through the valley, sending everyone indoors, rushing to shut their doors and windows. And when he slept, he snored louder than thunder. The villagers huddled in their homes, holding their heads and wishing Heavyhand would go away. But he wouldn't.

It wasn't long before they began to wish something else.

"If only Bulky were still big, he'd soon see off Heavyhand!" sighed one.

"It's our own silly fault," agreed a second.

"We shouldn't have been so selfish," said a third. "Bulky was such a thoughtful, kind and good-tempered giant. He never did anyone any harm!"

"We've learned our lesson. Let's get Bulky the Giant back!" said a third. So Spellbound was sent for again.

"Hm!" he said, stroking his long, grey beard. "I'll have to look up a growing spell. It might take quite a while to get it right!"

"We can't wait," replied Bulky, "Heavyhand is causing too much trouble. I've an idea! Listen carefully..."

As Heavyhand lay snoring in the shade, he felt something tickle his nose. It didn't stop until, snuffling and snorting, he opened his eyes. Now a lot of folk aren't in their best mood when woken suddenly. Heavyhand was definitely in his worst, especially when he saw a little figure laughing at him and waving a feather. It was Bulky.

"I tickled you!" he called cheekily. "Can't catch me!"

Bulky made a funny face and ran off, a split-second before a huge hand snatched at him.

Bulky jumped onto a horse he'd left nearby, and galloped towards the mountains, while a furious Heavyhand reached for his boots. But some of the villagers had tied the laces together and by the time Heavyhand had unknotted them, Bulky had reached the mouth of an enormous cave.

He didn't try to hide, but waited till Heavyhand had seen him before disappearing inside, with Heavyhand in hot pursuit! Bulky had found the cave long ago, during his days as a giant. He knew another way out, if you were small enough. Now, of course, he was! Bulky scrambled out into the fresh air.

The villagers were ready for their part of the plan!

As Bulky rode clear, they pushed against a rock high above the cave mouth, heaving and shoving until they set it rolling down the mountain, loosening others as it went, until an avalanche fell across the front of the cave.

Heavyhand had no time to escape.

"He's trapped inside!" cried the villagers.

But not for long!

How the mountain trembled as Heavyhand raged and cursed, as he began to dig himself out. He worked all day and night. So did

Spellbound, until at last his spell
was ready. The wizard's wand
whirled and he muttered strange
magic words. A dazzling arc of stars
appeared around Bulky who began
to grow and grow, just as
Heavyhand came bursting from
the cave.

Imagine his surprise when he
saw Bulky standing a good head
and broad shoulders above him.
Even for a giant, Bulky was big.

"Go and find your own valley.
This one's mine!" roared Bulky,
raising his voice for the first time in
his life.

None of the villagers minded
one bit. They were only too pleased

to see good old Bulky back to normal. Heavyhand took off nervously across the mountains without looking back.

"We promise never to complain again, Bulky," the thankful villagers told him. "We know we made a big mistake before!"

"More like a giant one!" someone joked and everyone laughed, though Bulky took care not to laugh too loudly!